Then he saved their lives, and they swore never to leave him.

We give you the Secret-Hairy-Snot-Tooth Oath of Devotion.

When he moved house, Billy found ANOTHER monster.

Hello. My name's Sparkle-Bogey.

One thing was certain – Billy's life would never be the same **AGAIN**...

Contents

Chapter 1
Big News

Billy burst through the front door and ran up the stairs to his bedroom. "I have **BIG NEWS!**" he announced to his Mini Monsters.

"What is it?" asked Trumpet.

"I'm going to **hospital**," said Billy, importantly, "for an **OPERATION!**"

What kind of operation?

"I'm having my tonsils taken out," Billy explained.

"Not your tonsils!" said Gloop.

Um, what are tonsils?

They're small lumps at the back of the mouth.

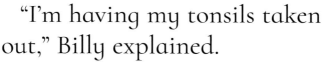

USBORNE

X091533

The item should be returned or renewed by the last date stamped below.

Dylid dychwelyd neu adnewyddu'r eitem erbyn y dyddiad olaf sydd wedi'i stampio isod.

Newport
CITY COUNCIL
CYNGOR DINAS
Casnewydd

PILLGWENLLY

To renew visit / Adnewyddwch ar
www.newport.gov.uk/libraries

Meet Billy...

Billy was just
an ordinary boy
living an ordinary
life, until
ONE NIGHT
he found
five
**MINI
MONSTERS**
in his sock drawer.

Gloop   Peep   Fang-Face   Captain Snott   Trumpet

"Yes!" said Billy. "And this operation is a **big deal**. I know it is, because after the doctor said I had to have one, Dad let me have an ice cream on the way home..."

With TWO scoops!

AND sprinkles!

"I wonder if we've got tonsils?" said Sparkle-Bogey.

The Mini Monsters decided to investigate.

"Can we come to the hospital too?" asked Captain Snott.

"**Definitely**!" said Billy. "I'm not going without you. My operation is in the afternoon, and then we'll be staying in hospital ALL night."

I'll pack your sock sleeping bags.

Hooray!

A hospital adventure!

I wonder if they'll have vegan cheese...?

"Will we get to go in an ambulance?" asked Fang-Face. "With flashing lights?"

"No," said Billy. "Mum's going to drive us there in the car. She's going to stay the night with me, too. The doctor gave us a leaflet all about it. Let's take a look."

11

Your Hospital Stay

How to prepare

You can have breakfast before 9am on the day of your operation, and water until 11am, but nothing after that.

What happens at the hospital?

When you arrive, you'll go to PUFFIN WARD. Before your operation, you'll be given an anaesthetic (say an-erss-thet-ik) , which means you'll be in a deep sleep when the operation takes place.

What happens during the operation?

Your tonsils will be taken out through your mouth. It usually takes 30 to 45 minutes.

After the operation

You'll be taken to the Recovery Room until you are fully awake, and then go to CROCODILE WARD where your parents or carers will be waiting for you.

You will be staying the night, but in the morning you can go home as soon as you feel better. You will have a sore throat for a little while, but you'll be given medicine to help with the pain. You will need to be off school for two weeks after the operation.

Why do they have **CROCODILES** in the hospital? That doesn't sound very safe.

"I don't think you can be there *during* my operation," said Billy. "But I'd really like you to be there when I wake up."

You can count on us!

We'll be there!

I'll be waiting with a big lump of cheese!

And I'll protect you from the crocodiles.

Before Billy could ask Gloop about the crocodiles, his sister, Ruby, called him down for tea.

Thank you! It's really good to know you'll be there with me.

As soon as Billy had left the room, Peep turned to the others. "We need to do everything we can to help Billy when he's in hospital. And I have a plan..."

In Billy's bedroom...

HOSPITAL MEETING

What's your plan, Peep?

I've found some books about hospitals. We should all study them.

And learn some doctor and nurse skills!

17

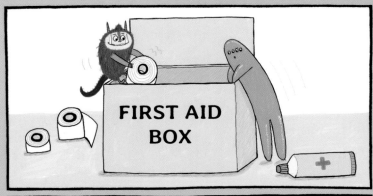

FIRST AID BOX

They won't stick!

I'm learning how to do a sling!

18

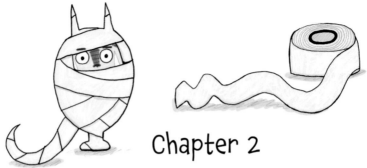

Chapter 2
To Hospital!

By the day of Billy's operation, the Mini Monsters had got much better at their doctor and nurse skills...

Billy had explained to Sparkle-Bogey that Mini Monsters **SHOULDN'T MAKE MEDICINES**. So she had made him a cake instead...

It's going to be delicious!

Sugar

Flour

Snot

Snot

Snot

Snot

Sparkle-Bogey's SNOT CAKE

"Now we're ready for hospital!" announced Captain Snott.

Billy was feeling ready too.
"Mum and I have made a list of
everything that's happening today,
so I know **exactly** what to expect."

1. Eat A LOT of breakfast as it will be my
   LAST MEAL for a looooong time

2. Pack my hospital bag

Make sure
Mini Monsters are
safe inside!

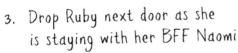

3. Drop Ruby next door as she
   is staying with her BFF Naomi

4. Drive to hospital with Mum and Dad.
   Ask Mum to drive as Dad's
   driving makes me feel sick

5. My operation is at THREE!!!!

So far, everything was going to plan. Billy's dad had made him his favourite breakfast.

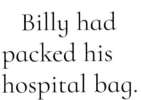

Billy had packed his hospital bag.

Mum was taking Ruby next door. Ruby had even given Billy a hug goodbye (Ruby didn't usually do hugs).

"So..." thought Billy, taking a deep breath, "that means it's time to drive to hospital."

His dad was waiting for him downstairs. "Into the car, then," he said, putting his arm around Billy.

Here goes!

Billy was surprised that his voice came out as a bit of a squeak. He hadn't thought he was feeling nervous, but **maybe** he was.

24

Or maybe it was just that he was REALLY hungry?

Billy checked his rucksack one last time, climbed into the car...

...and they **were off**.

Billy's mum and dad started talking to him. **A LOT**. Billy could tell they were trying to take his mind off things, but he wasn't sure it was helping.

"I know!" said his dad. "Let's put on some music."

Billy looked over at the seat next to him and saw all the Mini Monsters had started dancing.

"You don't have to worry," whispered Gloop, as they drew into the hospital car park. "We'll look after you." And he gave Billy's finger a hug.

The hospital was **bigger** than Billy had expected. It had lots of floors and seemed to reach really high into the sky.

Inside, they looked at the hospital map.

"We need to go to **Puffin Ward**," said Billy.

"Great," said Billy's dad. "Second floor, on the left. Follow the pink lines. We'll just get a coffee."

This place is HUGE!

Can we go and explore?

CAFÉ

Billy put the Mini Monsters gently on the ground. "Just make sure you're back in time for my operation," he whispered. "It's at **three**. And stay low!"

Slidy floors! My favourite!

"Ready, Billy?" said his dad, coming back with his coffee.

Billy gave him his best smile. "I'm ready," he said.

30

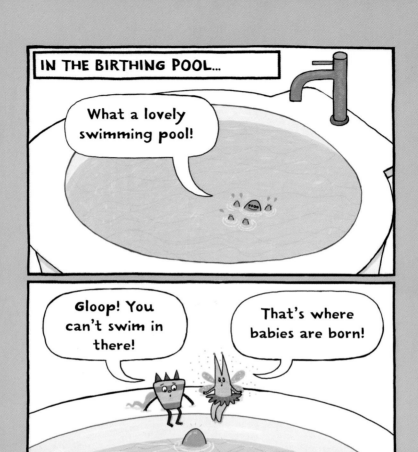

In the Laboratory...

Fascinating!

Time to get back to Billy...

Oh no! Where are all the others?

33

Chapter 3
Puffin Ward

A nurse will be with you soon.

When Billy and his parents reached the ward, Billy was shown to a little bed with a curtain. Billy saw the ward was full of other children, too.

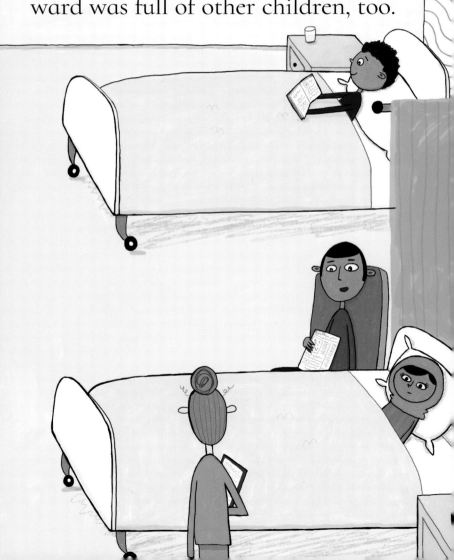

While they waited, Billy's dad started telling terrible jokes. "What do you call a fish with no eyes?"

I don't know, Dad.

A fsh.

Then they discovered that Billy's bed could move in all sorts of directions.

This is comfy.

Whoah!

Billy had almost forgotten why
they were there when the nurse came.

"Hello," he said. "My name's
Sam, and I'll be looking
after you today. I've got
a special gown for you
to put on. You'll be here
for about an hour and
then we'll take you in
for your operation."

"And here's a form," said Sam,
"so you can choose what you'd like
to eat when the operation is over."

DINNER

Name: Billy

Main (tick one)

☐ Roast chicken ☐ Fish fingers ☑ Veggie sausages

(tick one)

☑ Mashed potato ☐ Rice

(tick two)

☑ Peas ☑ Carrots ☐ Spinach ☐ Salad

☑ Apple crumble ☐ Banana ☐ Strawberry yoghurt

PUFFIN WARD MENU

When Billy had finished with the
form, Sam came back with some
cream. "I'll rub it on your hand, so
when you have your going-to-sleep
injection, you won't feel anything."

"I'll be back in an hour," said Sam, smiling.

"Why don't you go and look at the toys?" suggested Billy's mum.

Billy went over and found another girl looking at the toys.

"My name's Ella," she said. "I'm having my tonsils out today."

Billy thought about the tight, knotty feeling in his tummy. It was still there. Maybe it wasn't *just* because he was hungry.

"Actually, I'm a bit nervous, too," admitted Billy.

"After the operation, do you want one of my monster cookies?" said Ella. "My mum made them for me."

"Thanks!" said Billy, grinning. "Do you like monsters?"

Of course I like monsters! Who doesn't?

In that case, I'll show you my monster toys later!

Talking to Ella had made some of that tight, knotty feeling go away. Billy watched as the other children went in for their operations.

It's your turn next, Billy.

And that's when Billy realised...
HIS MONSTERS WEREN'T BACK.
"Oh no!" he thought. "I really need to see them. I'm not sure I can do this without them!"

43

Chapter 4
Operation Billy

It was time. A doctor had come to check on Billy and said he was ready for his operation. But as Billy was wheeled out of Puffin Ward there was still **no sign** of his monsters.

If only my Mini Monsters were here...

Billy couldn't help it. He'd started thinking of all the things that might have happened to his Mini Monsters.

Maybe they'd got distracted...

...or carried away...

...or trapped inside a **giant** machine.

But then Billy heard someone whispering his name. He turned... and there were his Mini Monsters!

"Wow," whispered Billy, as the monsters leaped onto his bed. "That was just like a superhero stunt!"

MP!

"Sorry we're late," said Gloop.
"You're going to be just fine," added Peep. "We'll be here waiting for you when you wake up."

"Thank you!" said Billy.

Then the Mini Monsters went to hide as a doctor came over.

"Billy, I'll be giving you the anaesthetic," she said. "And I'll be here all through the operation."

You'll just feel a tiny scratch.

Billy's dad held his other hand.
"Now count to ten," said the
doctor. "You can count in sheep if
you want to."

Billy smiled.

He knew *exactly* what he was
going to count in...

one monster, two monsters, three monsters...

He felt SO tired. "*Four monsters,
five monsters...*" And then, all of a
sudden, he was fast asleep...

Some time later, in the Recovery Room...

I heard the doctor say the operation went well.

What shall we do while we wait for Billy to wake up?

53

54

Chapter 5
Crocodile Ward

Once Billy was fully awake,
he was taken to **Crocodile Ward**.

I could get used to this!

Billy's mum and dad both gave him a **huge** hug.

"How are you feeling?" asked his mum. "Are you okay?"

"I'm still *really* woozy," said Billy. "And I was a bit sick at first, but I feel better now."

"Have one of my monster cookies!" said Ella.

"Thanks!" said Billy. "And *these* are my toy monsters."

They look very familiar!

"I'm sure I saw one of your monsters after my operation!"

"Only she was smiling... and flying," Ella went on.

"That is... **strange**," said Billy, peering at his Mini Monsters.

"I wonder how that could be..."

But before Billy could talk to his monsters, the food trolley arrived. Billy's mum put the food on a little table.

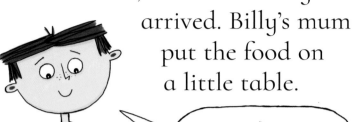

Just like a restaurant in bed!

"It's been a funny day today," said Sam, when he came round. "All the children are talking about tiny monsters. They're all saying they saw them in the Recovery Room."

I saw a pink one with wings!

"We've never had **anything** like it before..." Sam went on.

Billy's got some toy monsters.

They look like they could get up to mischief.

Actually, we're always finding them in funny places.

Then Billy's dad got up to go. "Time for me to pick up Ruby," he said, giving Billy a last hug.

"And I'll go out for some fresh air," said Billy's mum, "if that's okay? I'll be back in ten minutes."

Billy nodded. As soon as his mum and dad had gone, he turned to the Mini Monsters.

Everyone's talking about you!

We were cheering up people in the Recovery Room!

"We thought it would be nice for people to see us when they woke up!" explained Captain Snott.

"And look how happy it made everyone," said Sparkle-Bogey.

Billy shook his head and smiled. Then he noticed that Gloop was being very quiet.

"What's the matter, Gloop?"

"Crocodiles?" said Billy. "There aren't any crocodiles here!"

"Then why is it called **CROCODILE** Ward?" said Gloop.

"That name is just for fun!" explained Billy.

"For fun?" said Gloop.

"Crocodiles aren't FUN!

They're **TERRIFYING**.

It should be called Mini Monster Ward instead!"

"I agree," said Billy. "That's a much better name."

And when Sam came to check on him, Billy suggested it.

I think that's a great idea. I'll see what everyone else thinks.

By the time Billy's mum came back, Billy was in his pyjamas, ready to sleep.

His mum pulled out her chair so it turned into a bed.

"I'm proud of you, Billy," she said. "You've been really brave today."

Thanks, Mum!

Then Billy turned to his Mini Monsters. "Good night," he whispered. "And try not to get up to TOO much mischief tonight..."

That night...

I know **EXACTLY** where we should go!

Follow me!

X-RAY

69

Chapter 6
Home Again

When Billy woke up the next morning, he checked on his Mini Monsters right away.

They were all sleeping **peacefully**.

And when Sam came round at breakfast time, he said that Billy was ready to go home.

"Your throat will be sore for a little while, but you'll start to feel better soon," he said.

Billy packed his bag...

Bye, Ella!

Bye, Billy!

...and then, at last, it was time to leave.

"And look at this," said Sam, as Billy and his mum made their way out. "We really liked your idea for the ward name, so we've changed it."

Mini Monster Ward

Hooray! And thank you for looking after me.

As soon as Billy got home, his mum put him straight to bed.

"Remember, you still need lots of rest," she said. "Ruby, you can see Billy, but don't stay too long."

As Ruby sat down, Sparkle-Bogey brought out her cake.

Look what I made you!

Wow! Er... thank you!

"How was hospital?" Ruby asked. "It was an adventure!" said Billy. "And I made a new friend. But I couldn't have done it without the Mini Monsters."

"What's more," added Fang-Face, "they named a ward after us!"

Then came the sound of footsteps outside Billy's door. The Mini Monsters dived under the covers.

You'll never guess what I heard on the radio.

"The doctors at the hospital are saying that they've found mystery X-rays! They're of tiny creatures never seen before!"

"Amazing!" said Billy, winking at Ruby.

I wonder what they could be...?

All about the MINI MONSTERS

CAPTAIN SNOTT →

LIKES EATING: bogeys.

SPECIAL SKILL:
can glow in the dark.

SCARE FACTOR: 5/10

← GLOOP

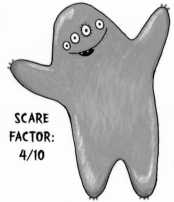

LIKES EATING: cake.

SPECIAL SKILL:
very stre-e-e-e-tchy.
Gloop can also swallow his own
eyeballs and make them reappear
on any part of his body.

SCARE FACTOR: 4/10

FANG-FACE →

LIKES EATING:
socks, school ties, paper, or
anything that comes his way.

SPECIAL SKILL:
has massive fangs.

SCARE FACTOR: 9/10

TRUMPET →

LIKES EATING:
vegan cheese.

SPECIAL SKILL:
amazingly powerful
cheese-powered parps.

SCARE FACTOR:
7/10
(taking into
account his parps)

PEEP

LIKES EATING: very small flies.

SPECIAL SKILL: can fly (but
not very far, or very well).

SCARE FACTOR:
0/10 (unless you're afraid of
small hairy things)

SPARKLE-BOGEY →

LIKES EATING:
eco-glitter and bogeys.

SPECIAL SKILL:
can shoot out clouds
of glitter.

SCARE FACTOR:
5/10 (if you're scared of
pink sparkly glitter)

11-01-23

PILLGWENLLY

Series editor: Becky Walker
Designed by Brenda Cole
Cover design by Hannah Cobley
Expert advice from Dr Stephen Farrell,
Consultant Paediatric Surgeon

First published in 2022 by Usborne Publishing Ltd., Usborne House,
83-85 Saffron Hill, London EC1N 8RT, England. usborne.com
Copyright © 2022 Usborne Publishing Ltd. UKE